The Gentle Beagle

Written by Karen J. Roberts
Illustrations by Lilith Jones

The Gentle Beagle

For Sebastanna Perez, Louise Perruccio, Dorothy Seaman
and Irene Roberts

chapter one

Deep in the woods of Virginia, in a log cabin, along a dusty road, there lived a hunter. The hunter was a gruff, grumbly man who didn't much care for the company of people. Alongside the log cabin was a red barn. The barn was meant for pigs, goats or cows. But instead, the hunter used the barn to house his only horse and his pack of hunting dogs. The dogs were Beagles, a breed bred for centuries and mostly used to hunt small animals. Beagles are very cute dogs with droopy ears and compact athletic bodies. Most Beagles have a white-tipped tail that stands up straight so they can easily be located in the woods. Beagles have an excellent sense of smell, and since they are hound dogs, they are very vocal, often baying together noisily. They use their vocal talents to alert each other and their master when they see prey. Beagles instinctually hunt in packs.

However, in this pack of dogs, there was one female who lacked that instinct. She was a gentle Beagle. She didn't enjoy hunting, and she felt bad for the small animals that were being chased and killed as part of the hunt. She felt kindness toward all living creatures, and even though she understood her packmates' instinct to hunt, she just didn't have that same drive.

Only one of the dogs was given a name by the hunter. The alpha male and leader of the pack was named "Duke."

The hunter relied on Duke to keep all the other dogs in line. He was the strongest and most agile of all the Beagles. He was also a good-natured leader who helped the weaker dogs by making sure they each had enough food and water. Duke was always the first one out of the barn for the hunt, and he stayed back on the return to make sure all the other dogs were safely back in the barn.

In the chill of early mornings, when the lights would come on in the log cabin, and all the dogs would stretch and stir restlessly in the barn, excited for the hunt that would soon begin, the gentle Beagle would feel anxious. She never wanted to join the hunt. The barn door would open, and she would hear the familiar heavy footsteps of the hunter as he saddled up his horse named "Zeus." Zeus was a big, muscular and fast horse, chestnut colored, with a flowing black mane and tail. Zeus loved the hunt because it gave him a chance to run through the grass and into the woods, and to breathe in the fresh air. He was always very friendly to the Beagles and felt protective of the pack. Running alongside them on the hunt, Zeus would pound his hooves on the ground thunderously. Being out with the Beagles was fun and exciting for Zeus, and sharing the barn with them made it seem like the dogs were family. The dogs kept him company, and he enjoyed watching them romp and play together.

Whenever the hunter saddled up Zeus, visible puffs of breath would appear from the big horse's nostrils as rumbling sounds came from his massive head. He would paw the soft dirt with his hoof, signaling Duke to round up the pack so the hunt could begin. But every morning, the gentle Beagle would feel more and more apprehensive because she knew the familiar command that would be booming loudly from the hunter's deep voice:

"Let's go, dogs! Time to hunt!"

All the other Beagles, barking, howling and blasting through the barn door with excitement, would leap over logs and race to the woods with great agility. The gentle Beagle would try to blend into the pack and act like she was hunting, but really she just pretended to. Even though this way, she would avoid hurting the small animals they were hunting, she still did not enjoy being part of the effort. In fact, she would feel bad just to pretend to scare and chase the ducks, rabbits, squirrels and fox they were expected to catch and kill on command.

After years of pretending to be a hunting Beagle, when really she was just a gentle Beagle, she finally found a solution. Each morning, when the hunter came in to saddle Zeus, she would hide behind the hay bales in the barn. In all the excitement and rush, none of the other dogs, or even the hunter, seemed to notice. This way, she could avoid the hunt, the one thing in life she was expected to do. Each day in the barn, she passed the quiet time without the other dogs by making friends with the field mice and the occasional rabbit who unknowingly hopped into the Beagles' barn. She would warn the rabbits to stay away when the dogs were there, and she would save some of her food for the families of mice. Meandering like a free spirit, she took in the smell of the wild flowers growing in the field behind the barn, watched the butterflies flutter in the air, and marveled at the tiny hummingbirds with their long beaks in the honeysuckle blooms. She forgot all about hunting and just felt happy being part of nature.

Duke, the alpha dog, knew she was staying back in the barn, and at first he pretended not to notice. He didn't want to make her feel bad, and since he was in charge of the pack while they were out, he had more important responsibilities to worry about. However, he really liked her gentle nature and wanted to protect her. Therefore, he eventually went out of his way to be sure she had a safe place to hide before the hunter arrived, and he made certain all the other Beagles knew it was okay for her to stay back in the barn. As the pack leader, the other Beagles respected Duke, and they began to feel equally protective of her.

Most afternoons, when the hunter was off running errands in town, or settled back into the log cabin for the day, Duke would rest in the hay next to the gentle Beagle. She made him feel calm, and he made her feel safe from the hunter. They would spend the lazy days together rolling in the cool grass, walking on the trails and smelling the scents in the woods. Of all the Beagles in the pack, Duke liked her the best. He would often try to impress her with his agility and strength, but he soon realized that she liked him for who he was on the inside. She enjoyed his company not because he was the strongest Beagle in the pack, but because she felt a connection with him. Her genuine friendship gave Duke a chance to relax and let down his guard when he was around her.

However, it was when Duke was leading the rest of the pack on a hunt, and the gentle Beagle was alone in the barn that she felt the most peaceful. Curled up in the hay, she would listen to the birds singing and the crickets chirping. Gazing through the door of the barn, she would watch the clouds moving across the crisp blue sky and would feel thankful that she was not part of the hunt. She knew she was different, and being different sometimes felt lonely. She wasn't willing to compromise her gentle nature, though, just to fit in with her kind. She knew she didn't really belong, but thankfully she had Duke to help keep her safe.

chapter two

One warm summer evening, while the other Beagles were off on a hunt, the gentle Beagle, found a cozy spot inside the bard to watch the sunset. Serenaded by the crickets, she watched, through the open barn door, the sky change to bright orange as the sun was setting. Feeling the soft breeze blow across the grass and into the barn, the gentle Beagle fell soundly and peacefully asleep. She awoke very suddenly to the flurry of the other Beagles bounding into the barn. She was so startled that she didn't have time to get back to her hiding place behind the hay bales. The other Beagles saw her and quickly tried to hide her in the pack, but it was too late.

The burly hunter had already seen her curled up, sleeping in the hay.

In a single, fluid motion he dismounted from Zeus and landed firmly and swiftly on the ground. Instinctually, all the Beagles took a submissive stance and put their heads down and ears back. The hunter marched up to the gentle Beagle assertively. She cowered, still in shock from the surprise of being jolted awake from her peaceful slumber.

"What do we have here?" asked the hunter, gruffly. "A lazy dog in the barn? Not hunting? Not pulling your weight around here, huh?"

He reached down and picked her up, staring her right in the eyes. He held her out for inspection.

"Lazy...and FAT! If you don't hunt, you get fat, and I don't have use for a fat and lazy dog," the hunter said, flatly.

Turning on the heel of his sturdy boots, he carried the gentle Beagle under his arm like a football. He marched out of the red barn and straight to his rusty pick-up truck on the dirt driveway. He deposited the frightened Beagle firmly on the passenger seat. Duke, who had returned to the barn after the hunter, had to watch in horror as all of this happened. He stood in front of all the other Beagles and watched sadly from the barn as the truck kicked up dust against the moonlight and sped away down the road. The dogs were still and quiet as they watched the truck's taillights fade into the distance. The crickets were still chirping, unaware of the terrible incident. That night, feeling responsible for what happened, Duke slept huddled together with the other Beagles. Even Zeus had a heavy heart and did his best to comfort the pack.

chapter three

The gentle Beagle stood, blinking, sneezing and coughing in a cloud of dust, while small pebbles sprayed in her face as the hunter quickly drove off in the pick-up truck. When the dust settled, and she was able to wipe her eyes with her paws, she looked around nervously.

He had simply opened the door to the pick-up truck, placed her on the dirt road and driven off without a second thought.

Slowly and carefully, she let her eyes adjust as she looked around. On the one hand, she was happy to be away from the rough hunter. On the other hand, she didn't know where she was, and she felt very scared. Tucking her tail, she nervously walked away from the road, but it was dark and her surroundings were unfamiliar. She saw a building with a single light on over the door. Cautiously, she made her way to the building, trying very hard to feel brave.

She felt totally alone for the first time in her life. She missed the red barn that she called home. She missed Duke and her pack of hunting Beagle friends. She missed Zeus, the field mice, the rabbits and the hummingbirds. Nothing was familiar. She had to admit, the hunter was right. She felt heavy and slow, and she had most certainly gotten fat.

She looked for a place to hide until morning. As she got closer to the building, there was nothing comforting about it. It was going to be a long and scary night before she would know what to do. She found an alcove, but it was dark. The ground was hard cement, not like the soft mounds of hay she was used to. She nervously kept walking around the building, looking for a patch of grass, when she heard a noise. She cocked her head to the side and perked up her ears, listening for the sound. She leaned forward, curious at what she was seeing.

She walked right into the side of a cardboard box, and the noise got louder. It was a box of kittens! They were meowing loudly, crying out for someone, anyone to find them. The gentle Beagle peered into the box to see four kittens on their hind legs reaching out and crying for her to comfort them. She gently turned the box on its side, curled into it the best she could fit, and let the kittens snuggle up against her warm belly.

The four little kittens, once crying and scared, were now purring together as they snuggled against the gentle Beagle. She was happy to have them to take care of. They were all still nervous and worried, but at least they had each other.

chapter four

The gentle Beagle and the four kittens drifted off to sleep, despite their scary surroundings and the occasional strange noise of a car driving by. The cardboard box was a poor excuse for a makeshift bed in this very strange new place, but they made the best of it.

Sound asleep and exhausted from their ordeal, they didn't hear the car slowly pull up to the front of the building. A man had come to the building in the middle of the night to pick up something he had left behind that he needed. He walked happily toward the door with a spring in his step, ready to retrieve his belongings, when he stopped dead in his tracks. In the soft glow of the moonlight, he saw the gentle Beagle and the four kittens sleeping in the shelter of a cardboard box turned on its side.

"Now what is this?" he asked, incredulously.

He slowed his pace and walked quietly back to his car. From the trunk, he fetched a bag of dog cookies and some cat food. As he approached the newly formed sleeping family, he quietly placed a few cookies on the ground for the dog, and a handful of food for the kittens. He was squatting in front of them, thinking about what to do next, when all of a sudden...

"Hooooowl!!!!!!"

"Woof, woof!!!"

The gentle Beagle awoke to the smell of the food and was very confused as to where she was. Startled by this stranger in front of her, she sprang to her feet and sounded her alarm. The cardboard box went flying, and the four kittens were so scared they ran in every direction until they were out of sight.

"Whoa, whoa there, little fella, it's okay! It's all right!" said the kind man. However, he also had been surprised by the sudden commotion, and so his voice was not as soothing as he had intended. He had fallen backward onto his hands and struggled to get back up on the gravely driveway.

The gentle Beagle found herself barking frightfully. The smell of the food was enticing, but she didn't feel comfortable eating it. She wanted desperately to somehow feel safe again. She heard the kittens crying and wanted to collect them from their hiding places.

Finding his calmness again, the kind man spoke quietly, offering up the food. He reached into the weeds that were against the building and scooped up one of the kittens, holding him gently and lovingly against his cheek and finally placing him next to the gentle Beagle.

Together, the kind stranger and the gentle Beagle gathered up the other three kittens that were relieved to be reunited. As they all calmed down as a group, they cautiously accepted the food and happily filled their very hungry bellies. All the fear and excitement had made them hungry, and they had had enough drama. Even though the gentle Beagle had never seen any human other than the gruff hunter, she was learning that they are not all bad. This one was kind, and not only offered her and the kittens food to eat, but he somehow made her feel safe. She slowly walked toward him, and he softly petted her under the chin, until she folded her body into his lap right there on the ground. He sat quietly petting her and the kittens until they all felt safe again.

chapter five

"Okay, little fella, let's get you and these kittens inside for the night," said the kind stranger.

He scooped up the kittens and placed them back in the box. As his keys jingled, the door to the strange building opened. He stepped back with the cardboard box in his arms and held the door open for the gentle Beagle to walk in first. Happy to be out of the scary, cold, dark night, she padded into the building.

Her happiness was short-lived when she heard the cacophony of barking and meowing all at once. She stopped in her tracks, tucked her tail and looked up at the kind stranger for reassurance because he was all she had.

"It's okay, fella, we just woke everybody up."

The gentle Beagle looked around and saw lots of cages lined up. Some cages had big dogs in them. Other smaller cages were stacked on top of each other with small dogs in them. She could smell the fear and the unrest, and suddenly she decided this might not be the safest place. The dogs were barking and crying out for food, or out of loneliness or fear. This was not a happy place. And then, she remembered who brought her here. It was the gruff hunter who said she was fat and lazy and that he had no use for her. He dumped her at this bad place to get rid of her.

The kind stranger tried hopelessly to comfort the barking dogs, but they continued to carry on. The lights coming on suddenly and the sight of a human made them want anything but the inside of their cages. She watched as he gently placed the four kittens in a cage together on a towel. Next, he scooped up the gentle Beagle into his arms.

"Oh, excuse me, I've been calling you 'fella!' Looks like you're a lady," he said to her in a sweet voice. "Let's see, you sure are a darling little girl! How about we call you 'Darla?' Does that sound okay? My goodness, Darla, you're a heavy girl. You've been eating too much, huh? Not getting enough exercise?" asked the kind man. She looked back at him, exhausted from the night, and realized she was just given her very own name, for the first time in her life. Darla. She liked the sound of it.

The gentle Beagle, now named "Darla," was placed into a cage on an old towel inside the strange building with all the other nervous and needy dogs and cats. The kind man gave her a final pat on the head and a bowl of water before he slipped back out the door and left the animals in darkness again. She was happy not to be outside, but somehow this wasn't much better. Tired from her ordeal of being abandoned, now in a small cage, unsure of her future, she finally drifted off to sleep as the other dogs settled back down in the darkness of the night. She hoped the four kittens weren't too scared.

chapter six

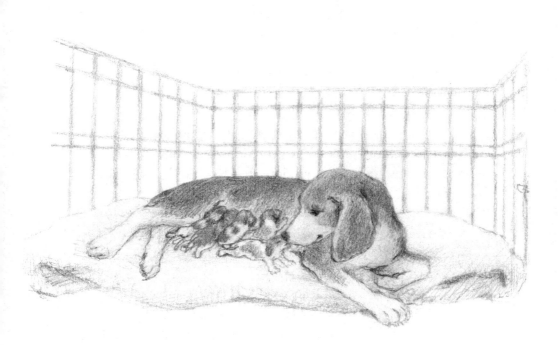

As the sun came up, two cars pulled into the parking lot of the building and parked alongside one another. As the women got out of their cars, holding coffee cups and lunch bags, they said "good morning" to each other and yawned.

"Another day in paradise," one woman said to the other.

They turned the key in the door, flipped on the lights and listened to the sound of the dogs barking and the cats and kittens meowing, anxious for food and any form of attention.

"Yeah, we hear ya! We'll get to you soon enough," the women said as they put down their belongings and began to get the food ready.

"What the heck?" one woman said confused and stunned. "Come quick, you have to see this!" she called out.

The two women, with their eyes wide and mouths open, watched in awe at what they were seeing. In the cage, the gentle Beagle was laying on her side with five newborn puppies peacefully curled up against her belly.

She wasn't fat or lazy. She had been pregnant. And during the night, she had given birth to five tiny puppies.

The woman looked at the tag on the cage.

"Darla. Her name is 'Darla,'" the woman said. On the desk, she saw a note left by the man who was there last night to let Darla and the kittens inside. "Looks like there are four kittens, too?"

The women were squatting down in front of Darla's open cage petting her gently as she licked her new puppies. Darla was enjoying the attention, when there was a sudden and loud interruption. A large man entered the room assertively, and the sound of his heavy feet and deep voice reminded her of the hunter. It wasn't the hunter, though. It was a new stranger with negative energy that Darla sensed immediately.

"What is this?" he questioned, loudly.

Darla felt the fur on her neck stand up in fear. The scary man bent down in front of the open cage. He snatched up one of her tiny, newborn puppies by the scruff of his neck, and the pup yelped in fear. Darla was no longer scared. She was experiencing an unfamiliar emotion. She had a sudden and strong urge to protect her babies from this threatening man, and the gentle Beagle showed her teeth and growled. This was something she had never done before, but her puppy was scared, and her instinct was to snarl and snap at the man.

"Whoa!" said the man, as he dropped the scared puppy back onto the others, pulling his arm back quickly.

"Aggressive. She's a biter. Put her on the list. She's got two days, and then we'll put her down. The puppies are too young. Unless you can find someone crazy enough to bottle-feed them in the next two days, they should go on the list, too. We just can't handle an aggressive dog, and we certainly don't have the resources to deal with these puppies. They all have to go," the man stated firmly and without emotion, as he closed the cage, stood up and went about his business.

The two women looked at each other, shrugged their shoulders and grabbed the clipboard. Following the orders from the man, they added Darla and her puppies to the list of dogs scheduled to be put down in two days and went about the long task of feeding all the dogs and cats in the cages.

chapter seven

Darla woke up to her five hungry puppies wanting to be fed. It was her second day at the shelter. The past 48 hours had been unbelievable. She was abandoned on the side of the road, leaving everything she knew behind, and now she was a mom to five small puppies, while living in a cage surrounded by strangers and other dogs in distress. She thought about how much her life had suddenly changed. And while she missed the soft hay of the barn, the smell of the grass, the sound of the birds chirping, and all her Beagle friends, she now had her puppies to think of. She had to make sure they were fed, clean, warm and safe. However, being in this environment was making her feel sad and hopeless.

Today, a new woman came into the building in the early morning, and she was kind and gentle as she reached in to give Darla food and water. She stroked her softly and spoke in a sweet voice, and she was careful not to disturb the puppies. Darla wished every human would treat her this way, but she was learning that not all humans are scary.

The nice woman took something out of her pocket and held it up. It flashed at her for a split second. Then, the woman softly closed the cage door.

"Hi, it's Deven, from the shelter. I'm sending you a picture right now. We have a momma Beagle and her five puppies. Today is her last day; they are all on the euth list for tomorrow morning. Is there any chance you can come today? She's a real sweetheart," she said into the phone. The nice woman named "Deven" squatted back down in front of the cage and said, "Don't worry, Momma, we're gonna get you out of here."

That afternoon while Darla and her puppies were taking a nap, a car pulled into the parking lot. The side of the car said "April Farm Foster Care" in bright blue letters. A man and woman got out of the car, carrying bags and boxes. They were dressed in jeans and sweatshirts with the same April Farm Foster Care logo on it. The bags and boxes were filled with blankets, dog toys, towels and food for the animals at the shelter. They tried to support as many shelters as possible, but this one was in a remote location, so they didn't make it here very often. Not many people came to rescue or adopt the dogs that ended up here. There were so many strays and unwanted, abandoned dogs and cats, all hoping for a new home. Unless someone came to rescue or adopt them, they would eventually have to be put down due to overcrowding. It was a very sad situation.

Olivia and Tyler were the owners of April Farm Foster Care. They started the program at their idyllic farm after their daughter, April, died from a rare form of cancer at the age of 18. April loved animals. So, to honor her life and to ease their pain and grief of losing their only daughter, they focused their energy on providing a safe and loving foster home for dogs in need. They were at the shelter to pick up Darla and her five puppies. The couple were going to provide them with a loving home environment so that the puppies would grow up to be healthy, happy dogs that would have the best chance to be adopted.

As Darla woke up from her nap, her hungry puppies wanted to eat again. She was sleepy, and it took her a minute to remember where she was. Again, she felt sad when she realized she was still in the cage. But she suddenly felt a wave of positive energy, as two people were sitting cross-legged in front of her, smiling at her with kind eyes. She felt no threat, just love. Darla put her ears back as she looked up at Olivia and Tyler. Her tail thumped against the floor of the cage as she wagged it for the first time since her ordeal started.

"Let's get you out of here, sweet girl. You and your babies are safe now."

chapter eight

Darla was sleepy, but her excitement started to take over as she peered out the window of the car. These two caring people had gently carried her and her babies out to a big comfortable dog bed with soft blankets in the back seat of the car where they now found themselves. Olivia kept turning around and checking on her, scratching her under the chin with her arm twisted in an unnatural position from the front seat. She was so concerned with her safety and comfort that Darla knew this woman was really special. With Darla's babies placed lovingly at her side, and the soft hum of the car moving farther and farther away from the shelter, Darla was filled with a feeling of comfort she had never before experienced. Tyler, the man driving the car, was turning slowly and carefully around the bends. They spoke to each other using calm voices, and satisfying smiles of happiness mixed with worry and concern for Darla. These were people she wanted to know; humans who made her feel love. Pure love.

They pulled up a long stretch of road to a cozy farmhouse on a grassy hill. There was a wooden sign on the hill that said "April Farm, Safe Foster Care for Pets." As they slowly drove up the long driveway, Darla could feel the energy change in the car, and she knew they had arrived.

Olivia and Tyler settled the babies into a soft playpen set up in front of a big sliding glass door that overlooked a beautiful grassy yard with trees for shade and plenty of room to play. Now that the babies were sleeping safely, Olivia scooped up Darla and hugged her tight.

"Welcome home, sweet Darla. You are safe now. Let's show you around. Don't worry, your babies are safe," Olivia spoke kindly and softly right into Darla's floppy ears as she carried her around the house.

"This is the kitchen where we'll feed you and your babies when they are a bit older…and this is where Tyler and I sleep, see it's right near your bed, so we can hear you if you need us. These are pictures of our precious April. She was our daughter. See how beautiful she was? We loved her so much, Darla. Oh, how she would have loved you. She just loved all animals. We started this foster farm in her honor after we lost her. All the love we had for her, and still have for her, has been for the animals, just like she would have wanted. And now that we have you and your babies, that love will be for you." Olivia gave Darla soft kisses on the side of her snout as she explained all this to her.

Darla relaxed into Olivia's arms and soaked up the love. She let out a long, content sigh as she realized she could finally relax. She was safe.

After Darla had a chance to play in the grass, rolling around happily, and exploring her new yard, she was ready to get back to her babies. And the babies were ready to be fed. Being a mommy was a full-time job, and Darla felt much happier about it now that Olivia and Tyler were there to help her. They settled into a routine that provided Darla and her growing babies with comfort and happiness.

And then one day, weeks later, when her babies were old enough to eat solid food and play on their own in the yard, a man arrived at the farm. And it was a hunter.

chapter nine

Darla watched from the window as the car door opened. First, she saw the familiar hunting boots and similar clothing. She put her ears back and lowered her head in fear.

"It's okay, Darla. Why are you so scared?" asked Tyler.

She looked up at him for reassurance and looked back out the window. When the man got out of the car and walked toward the front of the house, Darla realized it was not the same hunter who had dumped her at the shelter. This man wasn't burly. He had a kind face, and he carried himself in a friendly way. She started to feel less scared, but she didn't trust hunters so she was careful not to let down her guard just yet.

"Hi, I'm Jason. We spoke on the phone...about the Beagle pups," the hunter said to Tyler as they shook hands.

"Yes, hi," replied Tyler. "Thanks for making the trip out. Come on in."

Darla sat back with her puppies and watched the two men look around the farm and talk easily. The puppies were now much bigger and very playful. They were so much fun and Darla loved them, but they didn't need her as much anymore. Olivia explained to her that her babies would soon go off to live in their own new homes with their own new families, and although it would be sad to see them go, it was best for the pups.

Tyler opened the sliding glass door from the backyard, and their voices got louder as they stepped into the house. The puppies perked up their ears and all five of them romped playfully toward the door. They jumped up, knocking into each other, getting tangled together, barking to invite the visiting hunter to play.

The hunter squatted down, laughing happily as he let Darla's puppies jump all over him. They licked his face and tugged his sleeve, and finally, he sat cross-legged on the floor so he could interact comfortably. He was chatting with Tyler and Olivia about which ones were male versus female, the coloring of their fur, and, most of all, their temperament. When the puppies settled down a bit, satisfied with the attention they received, the hunter reached out to pet Darla who was sitting quietly a few feet away. She pulled back a little bit, sniffed his hand, and cautiously let him scratch her under the chin.

"She's a beauty," the hunter said to Tyler.

"She's a good momma. And the sweetest dog you could ever ask for," replied Tyler.

"Well, I think I'll take these three here," the hunter stated, turning his attention back to the puppies. "I need a few more in my pack, and the older dogs can teach them the ropes."

Darla rested her chin on the ground sadly. She knew she was a Beagle, and her puppies were Beagles, and that meant they were supposed to be hunting dogs. However, thinking about her puppies growing up to chase and kill small animals made her sad. She knew there was nothing she could do about it. The puppies had to find new homes. They had energy and athleticism, and they deserved a life doing what they were bred to do. But, it still made her sad.

She licked the three pups "goodbye," and they closed their eyes, snuggling into her one last time before bounding down the hall with the hunter to start their new lives. She pulled her last two remaining puppies close to her and gave them extra love and attention.

Tyler walked the hunter to his car and helped the puppies get settled in the crate in the back. Olivia gently sat down next to Darla on the floor and stroked her head. Darla rested her chin on Olivia's knee and listened as Olivia explained to her that this hunter was different from other hunters. He trained dogs to do something called "field trials" and "competitions." It meant that her puppies would grow up learning to hunt, but that they would use toys instead of small animals. They would have lives filled with fun, exercise and fulfillment of their instincts, without any other animals getting hurt. It was just for fun, she said. Darla felt so relieved. She drifted off to sleep in the comfort of Olivia's lap, dreaming of her three puppies growing up to be gentle Beagles, learning playful hunting just for fun.

chapter ten

In the next few weeks, Darla said "goodbye" to her last two puppies. Both went to nice families with young kids. She was happy for them and enjoyed watching from the window both times as the kids ran in the yard with the puppy while the adults talked about the adoption. As they drove off down the road away from the farm, the humans seemed so excited about getting their new furry family member home and settled. Knowing her puppies would be loved and safe gave Darla comfort.

It sure was quiet that first day after the last puppy had been adopted. Darla was happy to have Olivia and Tyler all to herself, and she settled in on the couch with them. She drifted to sleep listening to them talk softly while they gently petted her. With the droning sound of the TV in the background and her stomach full from dinner, Darla felt completely at peace. Her past ordeal was becoming a distant memory as she soaked up her quiet surroundings.

The quiet didn't last long, however.

Very soon after, Darla learned that Olivia and Tyler took care of lots of dogs. Once Darla's puppies had been adopted, they headed back out to the shelters to rescue and foster more dogs in need. Normally, it would be Darla's turn to be adopted by a nice family. That's what fostering was all about—finding homes for the dogs so more could be saved. But the truth was, Darla was such a special dog, Olivia and Tyler had already decided they would keep her at the farm as part of their family. They just couldn't part with her. She was home and wouldn't have to start over again with a new family. She became the resident dog at the farm, happily greeting potential adopters and supporting the foster program with her gentle nature. Her sweet energy and calm temperament was helpful to the homeless pets they brought to the farm. Darla was a valuable and loved member of the family.

Over the next five years, Darla welcomed six other female dogs with litters of puppies. She helped the mother dogs settle in, and did her best to watch the young, rambunctious puppies so the mother could rest. There were all different sizes and breeds, and once there was even another litter of Beagle puppies. Darla became used to the cycle of watching the puppies grow and become more independent, eventually being adopted by new families. She had her favorites along the way, and some puppies were harder to say "goodbye" to than others, but she always knew they would all eventually leave the farm for their own new happy beginning.

However, it wasn't always mother dogs and litters of puppies that came to the farm. There were injured dogs with casts to heal broken bones, and dogs that had surgery for one issue or another, wearing plastic cones around their necks to keep them from fussing with the stitches. Some of the dogs that came to the farm had just had an eye removed, or even a limb amputated. Darla was always there to help the injured dogs recover and heal. Olivia and Tyler rescued senior dogs with hearing or sight impairment.

Some dogs were very overweight, while others had been nearly starved to death before coming to stay at the farm. Olivia provided the proper diet so the dogs could rehabilitate and work toward adoptability. Some dogs had terrible skin infections that needed frequent treatment; others required medication for canine ailments, like heartworm or other parasites. Darla was always there to help the dogs adjust.

One hot July, there was a particularly sad group of small dogs that came to the farm. A national rescue group called Olivia and Tyler for help with a large number of small-breed dogs that had been suffering from severe neglect and abuse at a place called a "puppy mill." The dogs were being used to breed puppies that would be sold to puppy stores. The dogs in need were the mother and the father dogs that lived at the mill. They had never been out of their wire cages for their entire lives. Unfortunately, the condition of the dogs when they arrived at the farm was typical for puppy-mill breeder dogs. Since being rescued, they had already been to the vet and groomer and were being treated for parasites, dental issues, and ear, eye and respiratory infections.

Of the 85 dogs that had been liberated from the puppy mill, the rescue group asked Olivia and Tyler to take eight of the oldest dogs into the foster program at the farm. These eight dogs ranged in age from 7 to 10 years old. They had never known the loving touch of a human or the feel of a soft bed. They had never had the chance to play, go for a walk or do any of the things dogs love to do. Olivia, Tyler and Darla used their collective efforts of patience, kindness and a special compassionate touch with these precious dogs. As the hot summer turned to autumn, those little dogs began to put their past behind them. They learned that life really could be wonderful. Each one, slowly, at their own pace, found the ability to feel joy, sleep soundly in a cozy bed, play with toys, roll in the grass and finally experience love. In the comfort and safety of the farm, with the help of the gentle Beagle, the puppy-mill survivor dogs came out of their lonely shells.

Olivia worked tirelessly to find just the right family for each dog. Each one of these brave dogs went home to a caring, loving family that understood their special story. They finally had their very own happy new beginning after a lifetime of neglect and abuse. It was one of the most emotionally exhausting yet rewarding times at the farm.

But not all of the dogs that came to the farm were sick or injured. Some were perfectly healthy, happy and wonderful dogs that sadly ended up in the shelter or abandoned by their families. Coming to the farm instead of staying in a cage at the shelter was a safer option for the dogs, and it gave them a much greater chance of finding a new home. Darla helped the nervous dogs to feel safe, and she taught the hyper dogs to settle down in the house. She befriended the shy dogs and provided companionship for each and every dog. There was even the occasional litter of kittens that arrived at the farm, and they always reminded Darla of the kittens from the shelter that terrible night she was abandoned. Darla was a gentle Beagle, and she had found her true calling. Olivia and Tyler saved her from being put down in the shelter, and in return, Darla helped them save hundreds more dogs in the years to come. Her gentle spirit and kindness became an integral part of the success of the farm.

Being a foster dog was her job, and the gentle Beagle loved it. She was so thankful for the home Olivia and Tyler gave her. She was happy to help them carry out their goal of saving as many dogs as they could. She realized that being a foster family for pets in need was a very special and selfless role to play. She watched Olivia and Tyler provide love and comfort to so many dogs over the years, and each one was special to them. They would receive updates from some of the families, and holiday cards with pictures of the dogs in their new home. It was heartwarming to be part of such a generous effort.

Darla had spent five blissful years on the farm. She couldn't have been any happier. Her life was perfect; at least she thought it was. But one very special day, a new dog arrived and changed everything.

Tyler drove up the long driveway to the farm after a trip to the remote shelter to rescue a dog. The front door slowly opened as Tyler gently coaxed the new dog in. Suddenly, awoken from her nap, Darla raised her head to see the new rescue. As soon as Darla saw the dog walk slowly and nervously into the house, she knew who he was. It was Duke, the alpha dog from the pack of Beagles in the red barn.

chapter eleven

Darla's ears perked up as she trotted lovingly right up to Duke. She nuzzled his nose and looked him square in the eye with pure joy. Duke's expression changed from scared, to surprised, to happy in a matter of seconds, and he returned the snuggles. The two dogs wagged their tails, and circled each other joyfully, gently playing. Duke was overcome with happiness as he playfully howled, while Darla pranced around him, howling in return.

"Wow, you two know each other!" said Tyler. "Olivia, come see this!"

Tyler explained to Olivia that the male Beagle was left at the shelter by a local hunter who said the dog's name was "Duke." It was the same shelter that Darla had come from five years earlier. He said the old Beagle's hips were sore with arthritis from years of hunting, and he was no longer of use to him. Thankfully, Tyler saw him and knew he had to rescue this discarded dog. Now, seeing that Duke and Darla were old friends, he knew fate had stepped in to bring these two back together. Olivia and Tyler wiped away tears of joy through grinning faces, watching in disbelief, as the two reunited Beagles playfully interacted. It was miraculously lucky that Tyler had gone out to the shelter the same day Duke was there. Olivia and Tyler shook their heads and happily hugged

each other knowing what a special day it was for their
beloved Darla.

Duke and Darla instantly settled into an easy routine
and lived side by side at the farm, going for walks, lying
peacefully in the grass watching the butterflies, listening
to the crickets and enjoying each other's company. It was
just like old times, but better. They were inseparable best
friends, as they both grew old together. Darla helped Duke
as his hips became worse, and Duke provided companionship and love back to her. Olivia and Tyler continued to
take in other dogs, but they were always careful to give
Duke and Darla plenty of love, and their own space to enjoy their golden years together.

When Darla got sick a year later, Duke never left her
side. He took care of her and brought food to her bedside,
and gently licked and cleaned her face for her. She was
very brave when she knew it was her time to go. She just
couldn't hang on anymore, and she rested her chin peacefully on Duke's big outstretched paws as she drifted off
to sleep. She never woke up again. She was buried in the
grassy yard under her favorite tree. Duke spent every afternoon resting sadly on the grass where she was buried,
watching the butterflies and thinking of her. He missed
his best friend.

Not long after, when Duke's hips could no longer carry
him, and his body had grown old and tired, he made one
last trip to Darla's grave. He curled up on the soft grass in
the warm sun and drifted off for the last time. His body
was buried next to Darla's. Tyler and Olivia would show
their new foster dogs this special spot in the yard, and tell
the story of Duke and Darla, the Beagles who were best

friends, and never left each other's side here at the farm. They kept the memory of their daughter, April, and the memories of Duke and Darla alive as they continued their mission of providing safe foster care for pets in need.

acknowledgments

To Deven Soto: Thank you for inspiring the idea for this story that fateful day at Starbucks! Having an open and candid discussion about rescue sparked so many elements in The Gentle Beagle. Thank you for your dedication to the dogs in need in the rescue community, and for your support with my books. I am very grateful for your assistance and link to children in the classrooms and through your awesome Animal Rescue Club for kids.

To Lilith Jones: Thank you for your wonderful contribution to the book with your incredible illustrations. Seeing the characters come to life through your artwork was amazing. You are a true collaborator, friend and talented artist. Thank you for your love and devotion to the very misunderstood Pit Bull breed. Your precious Athena is a shining example of all the wonderful characteristics the breed has to offer.

Karen with Roxie the Chihuahua. Adopted from *Get a Life Pet Rescue*, Roxie is a certified Canine Good Citizen, and she accompanies Karen to classroom visits teaching children of all ages the joy of adopting a pet.

Photo by Melissa McDaniel

about the author

Award winning author Karen J. Roberts has been an animal lover and pet owner her whole life. She was inspired to write her first children's book *The Little Blue Dog* when she adopted her little dog Louie from the Northeast Animal Shelter in Salem, Massachusetts in 2011. Since then she has published 7 books promoting animal kindness and adoption. Karen's humane education program for ages 3 – 18 was developed to inspire leadership and animal advocacy in the younger generations. As an animal rights thought leader, an animal rescue volunteer and humane educator, Karen's mission is to raise funding and awareness for carefully chosen animal rescue organizations in a family friendly way. Her love of nature and animals is present in her stories, which provide engaging, age appropriate rescue themes and challenging topics. Karen earned her BA degree in English at Syracuse University. She lives in Wellington, Florida sharing her peaceful home with her six dogs and one cat.

To learn more about Karen, visit www.thelittlebluedog. com

Winner of the 2013 Indie Excellence Book Award in the children's fiction category.

First place and third place winner of the 2013 Feathered Quill Book Award in the animal/children fiction category.

Finalist in the 2014 International Book Awards in the children's fiction category.

Other children's fiction titles by Karen J. Roberts:

The Little Blue Dog

The Little Blue Dog Has a Birthday Party

The Little Blue Dog Goes to School

Too Many Dogs

Homeward Hounds

Other non-fiction titles by Karen J. Roberts:

The Little Blue Dogma – Louie's Dog Handbook for Humans

Coming Soon:

A Terrier's Tale

The Gentle Beagle

Pretty Paisley Parrot

Peanut Butter and Pumpernickel

The Mossy Lane

Illustrator Lilith Jones and her rescue Pit Bull, Athena, who is a certified Canine Good Citizen, are pictured here between two students in the art school in which Lilith teaches painting. Athena is warmly welcomed in the school, where she spends her time exchanging unconditional love, affection and delight with the students. During school lunchtime, Athena might be found politely waiting for a tasty treat from any student who is happy to share.

about the illustrator

Lilith has been an artist and an animal lover for as long as she can remember and is very grateful to be able to combine those two loves in her work as a mural painter and an illustrator who specializes in portraying animals and nature.

Once she adopted her dogs from her local town shelter, Lilith began to volunteer there in order to help the dogs left behind. Having seen the suffering of so many dogs, she felt a deep connection to the story of *The Gentle Beagle*. She was honored to use her artistic talent and rescue experiences to illustrate Darla's story.

Lilith lives on her native Long Island, New York, where she and her gentle dog Athena enjoy rambles at nearby beaches and woodlands as well as meet-n-greets with friends old and new in their town.

Look for Lilith's illustrations in Karen J. Roberts' *A Terrier's Tale*.

To learn more about Lilith's artwork, visit:

www.lilithjones.com

To learn more about Athena, and the Pit Bull breed, visit:

www.badrap.org/breed-history and www.pbrc.net/breed-info.html

about the photographer

Author and photographer Melissa McDaniel traveled the U.S. for the last five years to produce the photo book projects, a series of photo books, note cards, fine art prints, calendars and more, all raising awareness about issues affecting animals in the U.S. today, especially those animals who are mistreated or misunderstood. The 4-book series (Deaf Dogs, Rescued in America, Pit Bulls & Pit Bull Type Dogs and Puppy-Mill Survivors) was inspired by her deaf dog Sadie, who was adopted from a shelter when she was a puppy. A percentage of the proceeds from Melissa's book sales is donated to animal rescue & advocacy groups.

Karen was lucky enough to work with Melissa during two pet photography events benefiting local animal rescue groups. Melissa photographed Roxie and Karen during one of the events, and they will cherish the photos for years to come.

the plight of the beagle

- Karen J. Roberts

The inspiration for *The Gentle Beagle* came to me in an odd way. Before I moved to Florida in 2012, I was contemplating moving to Virginia. Having endured the cold Massachusetts winters for the previous 18 years I was looking for a milder climate. Always interested in getting involved in animal rescue, I began researching rescues in the Virginia area and was surprised to discover that hunting dogs were discarded each year after hunting season. I had no idea it was such a problem.

Although I ended up moving to Florida instead, the plight of the hunting beagles stayed with me. I have since seen beagles in rescue here in Florida that ended up in need after being accidentally shot while hunting with humans.

After writing *The Gentle Beagle* and becoming more connected with the beagle rescue community, I also learned that the beagle is the most commonly used dog in animal testing and research labs. The reason they use beagles for product and drug testing is because they have such a gentle and sweet disposition. Currently there are almost 70,000 beagles being used in labs across the US. They are bred for this purpose, live their lives in cages, and are subjected to many different tests and scenarios most of us would consider incredibly inhumane. The tests are very costly to tax payers, in the majority of the cases they do not advance science, and although we do share some biology with dogs, the results do not correlate well with humans. I was very surprised to learn that most household products we use each day were tested on animals.

I know its sad and daunting and disappointing, but there is something each of us can do! We are all consumers and we cast our vote about what matters to us by the choices we make and the products we buy. You can shop for cruelty free products and make your vote count. Imagine if all of us did this? Together, as a society, we can make a difference. I think the beagles deserve better, don't you?

To learn more about companies that still test on animals visit:

http://www.thevegetariansite.com/ethics_test.htm

To learn more about cruelty free products, visit:

http://www.leapingbunny.org

To learn more about beagles being saved from research labs and how you can get involved, visit:

http://www.beaglefreedomproject.org

many beagles abandoned as hunting seasons close

By EMILY W. SHEPHERD AFP Correspondent

As anyone involved in animal rescue in the Mid-Atlantic area or the South can attest, the first season of the year is not really winter, but "beagle season," at the end of hunting season. "If hunters have any respect for themselves, they should be proud of their dogs and want to keep them," said beagle owner Holly Callaway. "I don't understand any hunter who has dogs he or she wouldn't pick up after the hunt. All dogs can't be perfect, but they all have their good qualities and deserve to be taken care of." And while any responsible hunter does take care to pick up all of his or her dogs at the end of a hunt, not all hunters are responsible; invariably there are dogs left in the woods. "Years ago," wrote one beagle rescuer in Maryland, "my own first 'found' hunting beagle stood in the middle of a country road watching my car approach. "It was a cold, foggy Tuesday morning in February," the rescuer said. "She was an old, thin blue tick girl, gentle and beautiful in the early light. I opened my car door and she jumped in. Elinor, I named her, a name that means 'shining light.' Elinor had no tags, no collar, no tattoo, no microchip. We checked with local vets and animal control. Obviously no one was looking for her; I took her home with me." But not all lost beagles find a new home so easily. County shelters in

New Jersey, Delaware, Maryland, Virginia, find themselves inundated with beagles and other hunting hounds at the end of January and February, and often have to kill dogs just to make room for these new arrivals. "This is the time of year when we get an influx of beagles and hounds due to the end of hunting season," stated one Virginia county shelter in its weekly e-mail to rescue groups about its adoptable dogs. "This means the 'urgent' dogs will have to leave as we run out of kennels." Dogs that don't hunt well or are injured, ill, or are seniors, are the ones usually found as strays or turned in to county shelters. Some of these dogs have gotten lost inadvertently; some are intentionally abandoned, rescuers said. The person most often caught in the middle, of course, is the land owner or other good Samaritan who finds a lost or abandoned dog. Not everyone is in a position to keep a found dog, but many people are uncomfortable about dropping off a dog at an animal control facility, particularly in a high-kill, rural area, where the dog will most probably be destroyed or — in some states — sold to a laboratory for experiments. In fact, "retired" hunting beagles do make wonderful, loyal companions, if they can get to a safe, reputable shelter or rescue, rescuers said. There are beagle-specific rescues serving New Jersey, Maryland, Delaware, and Virginia. For help with beagles or to adopt a homeless beagle in New Jersey, contact Linda Forrest at SOS Beagle Rescue, 856-336-2520 or sosbeagles@juno.com; in New Jersey and other mid-Atlantic states, contact Joan Kerr at Penny Angels Beagle Rescue, 609-965-9476 or beagler534@comcast.net. Other possible rescues can be found online.

The above article was found on: http://www.americanfarm.com

facts and statistics regarding the pet over population problem in the us.

- It costs U.S. taxpayers an estimated $2 billion each year to round up, house, kill, and dispose of homeless animals. (USA Today)

- Over 56% of dogs and puppies entering shelters are killed, based on reports from over 1,055 facilities across America. (*National Counsel on Pet Population Study*)

- An estimated 5 million cats and dogs are killed in shelters each year. That's one about every six and one half seconds. (*The Humane Society of the United States*)

- Millions more are abandoned, only to suffer from illness or injury before dying. (*Doris Day Animal League*)

- In six years one unspayed female and her offspring, can reproduce 67,000 dogs (*Spay USA*)

- Less than 3% of dog guardians are responsible for surplus births (*Save Our Strays*)

- The perceived high cost of altering is not the problem, but the lack of education on its benefits. On average it costs approximately $100 to capture, house, feed and eventually kill a homeless animal - a cost that ultimately comes out of our pocket. Low cost spay/neuter services are far below that amount. (Doris Day Animal League)

- The cost of having a pregnant female can be much higher than the cost of spaying Seven dogs & cats are born every day for each person born in the U.S. Of those, only 1 in 5 puppies and kittens say in their original home for their natural lifetime. The remaining 4 are abandoned to the streets or end up at a shelter (*The Humane Society of the United States*)

- Each day 10,000 humans are born in the U.S. and each day 70,000 puppies and kittens are born. As long as these birth rates exist, there will never be enough homes for all the animals (*Spay USA*)

- The public acquires only 14% of its pets from shelters; 48% get their pets as strays, from friends, from animal rescuers, 38% get their pets from breeders or pet stores (*The Humane Society of the United States*)

- Only 30% of dog guardians are aware of the pet-overpopulation problem (*Massachusetts SPCA survey 1993*)

- In a study of relinquishment of cats and dogs in 12 U.S. animal shelters, 30% of the surrendered dogs were purebreds. The same study indicated that 55% of the surrendered dogs and 47% of the surrendered cats were unaltered. (*Journal of Applied Animal Welfare Science*)

the humane society of the united states provided the following statistics:

- Number of cats and dogs entering shelters each year: 8–10 million *(HSUS estimate)*

- Number of cats and dogs euthanized by shelters each year: 4–5 million *(HSUS estimate)*

- Number of cats and dogs adopted from shelters each year: 3–5 million *(HSUS estimate)*

- Number of cats and dogs reclaimed by owners from shelters each year: Between 600,000 and 750,000— 15–30% of dogs and 2–5% of cats entering shelters *(HSUS estimate)*

- Number of animal shelters in the United States: Between 4,000 and 6,000 *(HSUS estimate)*

- Percentage of dogs in shelters who are purebred: 25% *(HSUS estimate)*

- Average number of litters a fertile dog can produce in one year: 2

- Average number of puppies in a canine litter: 6–10

Made in the USA
Middletown, DE
02 February 2020